CHOOSE YOUR JOURNEY

MW01029467

CHRISTMAS CROSSROADS

Elizabeth Raum

journey**forth**®

Greenville, South Carolina

Library of Congress Cataloging-in Publication Data
Raum, Elizabeth.
    Christmas crossroads / Elizabeth Raum.
        pages cm
    Summary: "Take an imaginary look into the lives of characters who
may have been present at the birth of Jesus Christ. You decide what happens to the three main characters by making choices what to read next.
You can then go back and take another path to read a new adventure and
outcome"—Provided by publisher.
    ISBN 978-1-62856-046-6 (perfect bound pbk. : alk. paper) — ISBN
978-1-62856-047-3 (ebook) 1. Jesus Christ—Nativity—Juvenile fiction.
2. Plot-your-own stories. [1. Jesus Christ—Nativity—Fiction. 2. Plot-your-
own stories.] I. Title.
    PZ7.R195445Cf 2015
    [Fic]—dc23

                                                              2015012593

All Scripture is quoted from the King James Version. The Christmas story
is found in Luke 2. The account of the Magi is found in Matthew 2.

Illustrator: Zach Franzen
Designers: Elly Kalagayan and Chris Taylor
Page layout: Michael Boone

© 2015 by BJU Press
Greenville, South Carolina 29614
JourneyForth Books is a division of BJU Press.

ISBN 978-1-62856-046-6
eISBN 978-1-62856-047-3

15 14 13 12 11 10 9 8 7 6 5 4 3 2 1

For Adeline and Greta, with love

Contents

A NOTE TO PARENTS AND TEACHERS

This book is an interactive novel. Younger readers may be unfamiliar with this format. It invites readers to interact with the text by making choices as they read. The choice determines what happens next.

Readers must follow the directions at the bottom of each page (see "A Note to Readers"). Sometimes they simply turn the page. Other times they will flip ahead several pages. Readers can go back later to choose a different option to see how the story changes. Each story is presented in short segments. There are multiple paths and several endings in each chapter. This format gives young readers a sense of control over the text.

Although this book is firmly rooted in Scripture, it is a novel. It takes an imaginary look into the lives of characters who might have been present at the birth of Jesus Christ. Your child may notice that these stories vary from nativity pageants they have seen. A note at the back, "What Bible Experts Say," explains these differences. For example, in this novel there is no innkeeper. Mary and Joseph stay in a home. This idea is based on the work of evangelical Bible scholar Kenneth Bailey, who suggests in his book *Jesus Through Middle Eastern Eyes: Cultural Studies in the Gospels* that "inns" as we know them did not exist in ancient Bethlehem. Travelers stayed in the homes of relatives. If the "guest room" was full, then visitors were offered space in the family's main living area. Most homes probably had a stable area at one end. Animals were brought inside at night.[1]

Parents or teachers may want to discuss with young readers the topics in the "Going Farther" section that begins on page 121.

Reading should be an adventure. So should faith. We hope your child enjoys these adventures based on the gospel stories.

---

[1]Kenneth Bailey. *Jesus Through Middle Eastern Eyes: Cultural Studies in the Gospels* (Downers Grove: IVP Academic, 2008), 31–34.

A NOTE TO READERS
BEFORE YOU BEGIN YOUR ADVENTURE

Imagine that you were there on the night Jesus was born. What would you see? What would you hear? What would you do?

In this book you'll have the chance to find out. You'll have to make lots of choices. First, you must decide what part you want to play. As you read, you will make more choices. Your choices make a difference in what you see, hear, and do. Follow the directions at the bottom of each page.

When one story ends, you can go back and choose again. How will the story change if you make a different choice? There are many paths to follow. Each chapter contains several complete stories.

At the end of this book you'll find some special helps. A glossary defines words you may not know. You'll learn how to find these stories in your Bible. You'll also learn what Bible experts say about life 2,000 years ago.

YOUR FIRST CHOICE: WHO ARE YOU?

If you are a shepherd boy, turn to page 1.
If you are a girl of Bethlehem, turn to page 37.
If you are a boy from Parthia, turn to page 79.

A Shepherd Boy

Night has fallen. Sheep brush past you. Their soft wool rubs against your legs. Soon they will be safe inside the sheepfold. Uncle Eli begins counting them.

These sheep are special. They belong to the priests at the temple in Jerusalem. You watch the sheep day and night. They will be offered to God in the temple at Jerusalem. They must be perfect: no spots, no scars, and no bruises.

They'll be safe in the sheepfold. The sheepfold is a big circle. Rock walls surround it. There is only one opening. A shepherd sleeps in the opening. He is the door. No one can get in or out without going through him.

Uncle Eli is in charge. Several older shepherds work with you. You take turns watching over the flocks. The nights are getting chilly. Your wool cloak keeps you warm.

CHRISTMAS CROSSROADS

A shepherd's job is not easy. The wilderness lies just beyond the hills. Robbers hide in the wilderness. They steal sheep. Wolves live there too. Bears prowl, and snakes slither. Watch out! Even though you are a child, you make important choices every day.

A GREAT LIGHT

Suddenly a great light appears in the sky. It comes closer and closer. You duck and cover

your head. Other shepherds fall to their knees. Only Uncle Eli stands tall. He raises his rod. He is trying to protect the flock.

A voice comes out of the light. "Fear not."

Fear not? You're terrified! You lift your cloak to shield your face. But the light shines right through the wool. It is so bright that it hurts your eyes. Strange beings hover at the edge of the light. Are they angels? Did God send them?

A voice speaks: "Behold, I bring you good tidings of great joy, which shall be to all people."

Uncle Eli lowers his staff. He reaches out to you. You take his hand and stand beside him.

"For unto you is born this day in the city of David a Savior, which is Christ the Lord. And this shall be a sign unto you; Ye shall find the babe wrapped in swaddling clothes, lying in a manger."

The City of David? That's Bethlehem. "Did they say a baby?" you ask Uncle Eli.

Before he can answer, many voices praise God: "Glory to God in the highest, and on earth peace, good will toward men."

An instant later, the light fades. Darkness returns. At first everyone is quiet. But soon the shepherds begin to babble.

"Who were they?"

"They were angels."

"Yes. Angels."

"Sent by God," someone adds.

The men nod. "It is a miracle."

Everyone agrees.

"We must go to Bethlehem and find the child!" Uncle Eli says.

"Yes! Yes!"

"To Bethlehem," one man yells. Everyone begins to follow.

Uncle Eli stops. "We cannot leave the sheep alone. Someone must stay behind to keep watch."

To stay behind, turn to *Watching the Flock* on page 5.

To go to Bethlehem, turn to *Bethlehem* on page 8.

Watching the Flock

You step forward. "I'll keep watch." Uncle Eli has always called you *his good shepherd*. You will prove him right.

He smiles. He is pleased. The oldest shepherd, Tomas, offers to stay with you. "I'm too old to hike down the hillside in the dark," he says.

The rest of the men hurry to Bethlehem.

"When the light first came, I prayed to God," Tomas says. His hands are shaking. "'Preserve me, O God: for in thee do I put my trust.' Those are the words of King David. He was a shepherd in these hills long ago. God protected David. I prayed that He would protect us too."

Tomas falls to his knees in prayer. After a few minutes, he tries to stand. You help him up.

"I have faith. God will not let us down," he says.

The prayer has settled him. He begins counting sheep. "One, two, three, . . ." There are many more. When he finishes, he looks upset. "One is missing. It is the one you call Star."

Star? She's fat and fluffy. Her lambs are strong and healthy.

"I'll find her," you say.

You scan the hills for the missing sheep. The stars shine brightly. The moon is full. But you cannot see Star.

"Star!" you shout.

Wolves, lions, and leopards roam this land. Brown bears live here too. You must find Star quickly.

"Star!" you call again.

She knows your voice. If she hears you, she will come. Listen!

"*Baa!*"

"I'm coming," you shout.

You follow her bleats. You climb a rocky hill and kneel beside Star. Her hoof is caught beneath a rock. You tug on her leg. She begins to bleat, so you stop.

Maybe you can use your long wooden staff to pry up the rock. You push the end of the staff under the stone. And then you lean on the other end.

"*Grrr.*" A gray shadow moves nearby.

A wolf! His blood-red eyes shimmer in the starlight.

Hurry! You must save Star. You throw all your weight onto the staff. The rock shifts. Star pulls free.

The wolf slinks closer. Your heart pounds. Your throat is dry. There is no one nearby to help you. Should you fight the wolf or grab Star and run?

To fight the wolf, turn to *The Sling Shot* on page 11.

To run with Star, turn to *Racing the Wolf* on page 29.

Bethlehem

Tomas steps up. "I'll stay," he says. "I'm too lame to walk to town."

"I'll stay too," his son Daniel says. "We will protect the sheep."

Uncle Eli leads the way to town. "We'll go to my home first," he says. "Aunt Susanna is the village midwife. She will know if a child has been born in Bethlehem."

"Yes," she says. "A baby was born tonight. His parents are from Nazareth. They came to be counted."

Caesar Augustus has ordered a census, or count, of the people.

"Go to the home of Caleb the stoneworker," Aunt Susanna says. "Joseph and his wife, Mary, are staying there. That's where you will find the child."

Your sandals slap loudly on the quiet streets. A light shines through the high windows of Caleb's house.

Uncle Eli knocks on the door.

Caleb opens the door a crack.

"The Lord be with you. It is I, Eli, who tends the temple sheep."

"Ah, Eli. Your wife was here earlier."

"Yes. I have spoken with her. Angels sent us to see the newborn baby."

Caleb turns away for a moment. Another man says, "Let them in."

The door swings wide. Uncle Eli enters. He looks around. And then he turns back to you. "The space is small. We will take turns."

Uncle Eli goes inside. Some of the shepherds follow him. Finally, it is your turn. You go to the far end of the house. Caleb's animals stay here every night. The baby and his parents are resting near the animals. The cows moo softly. The goats say *maa, maa.*

The child is wrapped in strips of cloth. He is lying in a manger. You fall to your knees. The angel called this child the Savior, Christ the Lord! He's just a tiny baby now. Is he a promise of great things to come?

Uncle Eli speaks to the baby's parents. "An angel told us that we would find the baby wrapped in cloths and lying in a manger. And it is so!"

The child wakes. His mother, Mary, lifts him up and holds him in her arms.

"It is time to go," Uncle Eli whispers.

You step out into the night. "Praise be to God," Uncle Eli says.

The others are waiting for you.

"Go to your homes in the village," Uncle Eli tells them. "We will return to the hills in the morning. Good night."

By morning the village is alive with news of the angels' visit. Each shepherd told at least one person. That person told another. Soon everyone has heard about the angels.

After breakfast you say goodbye to Aunt Susanna. You climb the hills above the village.

"It is a new day," Uncle Eli says. "We have work to do."

Some shepherds will take the sheep into the hills to graze on fresh grass. Others will take sheep to Jerusalem. There is work for everyone.

To go into the hills, turn to *Beside Still Waters* on page 14.

To go to Jerusalem, turn to *The Temple* on page 15.

The Sling Shot

You cannot outrun a wolf—not carrying Star. Maybe you can scare him away. You let go of the rod and reach for your sling. You have many sharp stones in your pouch. You load the sharpest one into the sling's leather pad. You twirl the sling round and round. It builds up speed.

You fire the rock straight at the wolf.

The wolf snarls.

You reload the sling and shoot again.

This time, the wolf yelps. You hear a soft thud and then silence.

What happened? You don't wait to find out. You grab Star and run.

Tomas is waiting. "You found her," he says. "Why are you out of breath?"

"A wolf!" You tell him what happened.

"You did well," he says. "God is watching over us."

The night passes without any more trouble.

The next morning you return to the spot where you last saw the wolf. There's a small cliff nearby. You look down. The wolf lies dead at the bottom. The rock scared him. He ran and fell over the cliff. The fall killed him.

Uncle Eli returns with news. "We found a newborn baby lying in a manger. We bowed down and prayed. Now it is your turn to see him. Stop and say hello to Aunt Susanna. Then you must go see the child that the angel announced."

You stumble down the hill to town. Aunt Susanna is waiting for you. She gives you cheese and bread to eat. Tasty!

"I suppose that you've come to see the baby?" she says. "The one that the angels proclaimed?"

"I came to see you!" you say. That makes Aunt Susanna smile. But she knows that you are eager to find the baby.

"The shepherds told everyone about the angels' visit," she says. "Everyone is talking about it. Many people have gone to see the child. They see what I see—a perfectly healthy baby boy. Not a king. Not a Savior. Maybe God is playing a joke on us."

You're shocked. And then you notice that Aunt Susanna's eyes are laughing. She grins at you. "Go on. The child is at the house of Caleb, the stonemason. When you come home, I have an errand for you."

To do the errand first, turn to *The Twins* on page 19.

To go see the baby, turn to *Visit the Baby* on page 25.

Beside Still Waters

Uncle Eli divides the flock into smaller herds. "Keep them away from swift waters," he says. "And be careful; there are reports of bears in the hills."

You guide your small herd slowly along a mountain pass. You reach a grassy pasture beside a small pond. Caves dot the nearby hillsides. The sheep graze near the water. They stop from time to time to take a drink.

You sit on a clump of soft grass and lean back against a small tamarisk tree. The sun makes you sleepy. Soon you drift to sleep. The sheep's bleating startles you. They sound scared. You jump up and search the shadows. Something moves near a small clump of trees. It's a brown bear!

To pelt the bear with stones, turn to *Battling the Bear* on page 17.

To take the sheep to the cave, turn to *The Safe Cave* on page 31.

14

The Temple

"I want you to go to the temple market with Ezra," Uncle Eli says. "Help him take the sheep to Jerusalem."

Thousands of people fill the city streets. Jerusalem is always crowded. Merchants sell their wares: pots in all shapes and sizes, cloth in beautiful patterns, spices, and jewelry. You pass vegetable stalls. Merchants sell beans, lentils, leeks, and onions. Baskets hold juicy melons. Colorful gourds swing from ropes made of woven goat hair. In one stall a man roasts fish over hot coals. Your stomach grumbles. But you pass by. You must get the sheep to the temple.

You enter the temple through the Sheep Gate. You lead the sheep to a pool and wash the dust from their coats. Soon a priest arrives. He inspects the sheep. Are they perfect? The priest nods.

Next the sheep go to the temple market. Jews coming to worship buy them as an offering to God. You used to worry that the sheep would suffer. But the priests kill them quickly. Blood splashes onto the altar. The fat is burned in the offering. The meat is not wasted. People eat it.

Ezra sells the sheep quickly. "It is a good day to go to the temple," he says. "We will praise God for sending us angels." He crosses the temple courtyard.

Suddenly Ezra stops. "There is Simeon," he says. "Simeon is a faithful man. He is my brother's friend. I must speak with him. Join us."

But a very old woman waves to you. "Come here!"

To stay with Ezra, turn to *Simeon* on page 24.

To go to the woman, turn to *Anna* on page 33.

16

Battling the Bear

You take out your sling. You pull some stones from the goatskin bag around your neck. As you do, you recall the words of the Psalm: "God is our refuge and strength, a very present help in trouble. Therefore will not we fear."

"Please, God, help me," you pray. Your stones look tiny, and the bear is so big. She is pacing at the base of a cliff. She is getting closer to the sheep. You take aim and twirl the sling. You shoot.

She roars.

You fire stone after stone at the bear. She rears back. At last she takes off into the hills. You fall onto the grass, but only for a moment. The bear may return.

You call to the sheep. They know your voice. They gather around you. It's time to return to the sheepfold.

When you tell the other shepherds about the bear, they cheer.

"It was good luck," you say.

"Oh, no," Uncle Eli says. "It was not luck. God protected you. Thank God."

You thank God for saving your life. You offer praises for His many blessings. You have lots of time to pray as you watch the flocks.

Turn to *Miracles* on page 35.

The Twins

"I'll do the errand first," you say. "Just tell me what you need." The errand won't take long. After all, Bethlehem is a small village.

"My water jug is cracked. I need a new one," Aunt Susanna says.

The potter's shop is not far. He has many new jugs on his shelves. It is almost impossible to repair an earthen jug. It is better to buy a new one.

You greet the potter and select a jug. You begin walking home. Two boys about your age stop you.

"Shepherd," they say, "move over. Give us room to pass."

You know them. They are twins. Their father is a rich landowner. Their home is at the edge of the village. Why should you move aside? Is it because they are rich and you are not?

To move aside, turn to *Moving Aside* on page 20.

To refuse to move, turn to *Standing Firm* on page 22.

Moving Aside

You don't want to fight. It is better to move aside. As the twins come near, they spit at you. They want to fight!

"You think you are special because an angel spoke to you," one snarls. "We heard all about it. The angels must have gotten lost. They should have come to our house."

His brother steps up. "We are the ones God favors." He juts out his chest. He wants you to see his fancy shirt. He lifts a foot to show off a fine leather sandal. Then he glances at your worn ones. "You are just a shepherd. You are nothing."

You are tempted to speak, but you do not. You wait quietly for the boys to pass. Uncle Eli has taught you well. Scripture serves as your guide. You remember these wise words: "Walk in the way of good men, and keep the paths of the righteous."

Your path is sunny. You intend to follow God's teachings. How can you do anything else? The boys are right about one thing. You are a simple shepherd. But the angels came to you. God loves all His people. God loves you. You will trust God forever.

Now it is time to see the baby.

Turn to *Seeing Jesus* on page 27.

Standing Firm

You smile at the boys, but you stand firm.

"Move aside," one says.

When you refuse, one of the twins pushes you. "I said move."

You grip the end of the rod hanging from your sash. It is heavy. A hard blow can kill a wild animal. It could hurt this wolf in boy's clothing, too. But you let your hand drop to your side.

When the boy pushes you again, you hit back. Your fist slams into his right cheek. Ouch! Your hand stings.

The boy begins to wail. His twin brother jumps you from behind. He knocks you to the ground and holds you down. His brother beats you on the head.

The potter comes running. He pulls the boys off you. The potter glares at the twins. "Go home," he says.

They spit on you, and then they slink away.

Blood runs like tears through the dust on your check. You wipe it away.

The potter helps you up. He gives you a new jug to replace the one that lies in pieces nearby. "Take care," he warns. "Everyone has heard of the angels' visit. Some people are jealous. 'Why shepherds?' they ask. 'Why not us?' But no one can understand the mind of God. Go in peace," the potter says. "God be with you."

"And with you," you say. You race back to Aunt Susanna with a smile on your bloodied face. She helps you clean up, and then you run to Caleb's house to see the baby. As you go, you smile. You know that God goes with you. God watches over you. The angels came to you and said that the Savior was for all people. All people. Even shepherds.

Turn to *Seeing Jesus* on page 27.

Simeon

"Stay with me," Ezra says. He tells Simeon all that has happened.

"The angel said that this child was the Christ child?" Simeon asks. "Are you certain?"

"Yes. Ask the boy."

You nod. "It is true."

"God be praised," Simeon says. "The day is at hand. The Holy Spirit told me that I would not die before I have seen the promised Savior." Simeon praises God. His joy touches everyone nearby.

You leave the temple filled with hope. For the rest of your days, you feel a deep joy. God sent the good news to you. He sent Christ the Lord to save His people. Praise God!

THE END

Visit the Baby

You race through the winding streets to Caleb's house. You knock on the door. Caleb steps outside. "Peace be with you."

"And with you," you say. "I have come to see the baby. The angels told us about him."

"Were you here last night?"

"No, I stayed with the sheep. Now I am doing as the angel commanded."

"Come inside." Caleb leads you through the house to where the baby is sleeping. He lies in a manger filled with sweet-smelling straw. His mother sits nearby. The father watches over them.

You bow to the mother and nod to the father. And then you peek into the manger. The baby is tiny. He's so new. Is he really special? That's what the angels said.

You only stay for a minute. You say a prayer for the baby. "Please, God, watch over him." The angel said that this baby is a gift, a gift to the world. The thought makes you smile. A gift? What does that mean? You will think about it as you tend the sheep in the days to come.

But now, you race through the village streets to Aunt Susanna's house. You'll do her errand and then go back to the sheep. A shepherd's work is never done.

Turn to *Miracles* on page 35.

Seeing Jesus

Aunt Susanna said you would find the baby at the home of Caleb, the stonemason. Joseph, the father, is Caleb's kinsman.

Caleb's house is built into the hillside. It is warm in winter and cool on hot summer days.

"Peace be with you," Caleb says when he opens the door. "Your uncle was here last night. He spoke of angels who praised God. He said angels sent him here. Did you see angels too?"

"Yes. But I stayed behind to watch the sheep."

"Come in," Caleb says. He swings the door wide and motions you inside. Villagers fill the simple home. Some are family. Some are neighbors or friends. They gather around a manger stuffed with straw. The manger is for the animals that come inside at night. Now that it is daytime, the animals are grazing outside. And a baby lies in the manger!

The baby is sleeping.

"What a fine boy," a woman says.

"He is so sweet," says another.

One very old woman offers a blessing: "The Lord bless thee, and keep thee: the Lord make his face shine upon thee, and be gracious unto thee."

The baby reminds you of the newborn lambs. They are tiny and weak. You do your best to protect them. Who will protect this child?

His mother watches him. Joseph, her husband, stands nearby.

You do not stay long. Others are waiting to come in.

When you return, Aunt Susanna gives you a hug. She offers you bread. It is still hot from the oven. Yum!

When you return to the hills, Uncle Eli asks, "Did you see the baby?"

"Yes."

"Do you believe he is the promised Savior?"

You think for a minute. "I do!" you say. Many babies are born every year in Bethlehem. But angels do not announce their birth. God sent angels for this baby and for this baby alone.

Turn to *Miracles* on page 35.

Racing the Wolf

You lift Star into your arms. She's heavy. You hold her against your chest. Then you run toward the sheepfold.

The wolf chases you. He huffs and puffs. He gets closer and closer. Then he leaps. His sharp claws sink into your back.

You wrap your body around Star. It's your job to protect the sheep. You reach for the club hanging from your belt and pull it free. You strike the wolf again and again with the hard wooden club. Finally he slinks away, leaving a trail of blood.

You roll onto your back. Stars shine down on you. Blood soaks your cloak. Is it Star's? No, it is yours. Suddenly you feel sleepy. Your energy seeps onto the hillside along with your blood. Star licks you. She nuzzles your face.

"What?" She startles you. You wake up. "I must get up," you tell yourself. If you stay where you are, you will die on the hillside beneath a blanket of stars. You pull out your reed pipe and play a few notes.

Tomas hears you. He hobbles over to where you lay. "God help us," he says. He presses his cloak against your cuts to stop the bleeding. He cares for you through the long night.

The other shepherds return to the hillside in the morning. Uncle Eli and Daniel, another shepherd, carry you to town. You have many deep cuts, but you will recover. Aunt Susanna is a healer. She will nurse you back to health. It will take months.

You never see the child that the angels foretold. By the time you are well, his family has moved on. But you often think about the angels' visit.

God gave you a special role that night. You were His good shepherd. You were ready to lay down your life for your flock. You spend the rest of your days watching over the temple flocks. You pray often. God's words give you strength: "Surely goodness and mercy shall follow me all the days of my life: and I will dwell in the house of the Lord forever."

THE END

The Safe Cave

You fear that your stones won't be much use against a bear. If only you had a stout wooden club like Uncle Eli's. It is studded with sharp pieces of metal. That's a weapon to use against a bear. But you're on your own.

You call to the sheep. They gather around you and follow you toward the cave. Caves make good shelters when the sky turns dark and bolts of lightning shoot toward the ground.

This cave is dark. The sheep hang back. You call them again. They follow you inside. *"Baa! Baa!"* The sheep flock together.

Shh! What's that other sound? It sounds like a baby crying. Why would a baby be in the cave?

Uh-oh! That's not a baby human. It's a baby bear! The bear outside must be the mother.

"Out!" you shout and push the sheep out of the cave. A mother bear is dangerous. She will fight to get to her cubs.

The sheep scatter. They run into the fields. One or two linger behind. You dash back into the cave to push them out. It's too late!

The mother bear rushes into the cave. She charges you. Her giant claws scratch your face and neck. You try to push her off, but she weighs five times what you do. She's crushing you. Your last words are a prayer: "Keep the sheep safe, Lord." And then you black out.

Another shepherd finds your flock that night. Two lambs are missing. The rest are safe. The next day, Uncle Eli finds your body. It is where the bear dragged it, near the tamarisk tree beside the still waters.

THE END

Anna

"Go to the woman. See what she wants," Ezra says.

Her name is Anna. "I am 84 years old. I have seen much in my life," she says. "I never leave the temple. I worship God day and night. I heard that angels came to the shepherds. Tell me, is it true?"

"I saw the angels myself," you say.

"What did they tell you?"

"That the Christ child was born in Bethlehem."

Anna falls to her knees in prayer. "Then it is so," she says. "Go in peace."

"And you also," you say.

You are quiet on the trip home. There is much to think about. How can a baby save God's people? You do not know. But God sent angels with news of this child's birth. He must be special.

Many years pass. You marry and have children of your own. One day you hear rumors of a man called Jesus. He heals lepers and gives sight to the blind. People say that he was born in Bethlehem. You laugh out of sheer joy. You have no idea what other miracles he may perform, but you know for certain that he is Christ the Lord!

THE END

Miracles

Many years later, you hear about a teacher who performs miracles.

"He gives sight to people who are blind," someone says.

"He is a friend to taxpayers."

"He tells wonderful stories," says another.

"He says that God is his Father."

Could this be the child born in Bethlehem? Yes! You repeat the words of the Psalm: "O my God, I trust in thee."

THE END

JOURNEY 2

A Girl of Bethlehem

Bethlehem is a small village. You know everyone, and they know you. Your father is a potter. Your older brothers leave early every morning. The rabbi teaches them the Bible. After school they work with Papa. They will be potters too.

Girls do not go to school. You stay home with your mother. She teaches you how to cook, weave, and care for a home. These skills will help you be a good wife and mother. Mama teaches you to love the Lord and to honor His ways. Even though you are a child, you make important choices every day. What you decide makes a difference.

Tabitha, your best friend, lives next door. She has two younger brothers. Samuel is four. Jacob is two. You help Tabitha watch them. Sometimes you feel like one big family. You call Tabitha's parents Aunt Martha and Uncle Caleb. A small courtyard separates your houses.

Bethlehem is crowded today. "It's the census," Mama says. "The Roman ruler, Caesar, wants a count of all the people in his empire. He has ordered everyone to return to the city of his birth." King Herod enforces Roman laws. If people don't obey, Herod puts them in jail.

VISITORS

Bethlehem is too small to have an inn, but most homes have a guest room where visitors can stay. There are two old uncles staying at your house. They arrived two days ago. Papa washed the dust from their feet. Mama served them her best dishes. They may stay for several weeks.

Tabitha's family has company too. An aunt and uncle are in the guest room. After supper, Tabitha runs into the courtyard. You and Mama are weaving beneath an olive tree.

"We have more guests!" Tabitha says.
"Joseph and Mary have come from Nazareth.
Joseph is a kinsman. Mary is going to have a
baby."

"Where will they stay?"

"With us. By the stable." The stable is at one
end of the family's main room. Every night the
animals come inside.

"Will Mary give birth soon?" Mama asks.

"Oh, yes!" Tabitha says. "Very soon."

"Then she will need privacy. You and your
brothers must stay with us. Papa and the boys
can sleep at the pottery shop for a few days."

What a good idea! It will be fun to have
Tabitha sleep over.

"The house *is* getting crowded," Aunt Martha
admits. "But we never turn away family. Thank
you for your offer."

Tabitha and her brothers spend the nights at
your house. You spread your sleeping mats next
to one another. Samuel and Jacob snuggle up to
you. You fall asleep to a gentle animal lullaby.
Sheep *baa*, goats *bleat*, and oxen *moo*.

Every morning you go to the well for water. Later you bake bread. You sweep the stable, milk the goats, and put fresh hay in the mangers. Tabitha is busy too. Before bed you play checkers and other games.

GET THE MIDWIFE!

A few days later, Tabitha rushes into the courtyard. "The baby is coming! I must get Susanna." Susanna is a midwife. She helps women give birth. "Come with me," Tabitha says.

You race through the twisty streets to Susanna's house. When Susanna comes to the door, you bow to show respect.

"Is it time?" she asks.

"Yes."

Susanna limps up the hilly street beside you. "Children are a gift of God," she says. When you reach Tabitha's house, Susanna hurries inside.

You try to follow, but Mama blocks the way. "The house is small. It is crowded," she says.

Several neighbor women have come to pray for the mother and baby.

"We have work to do," Mama says. "Who will put Samuel and Jacob to bed? Who will heat water for the baby's bath?"

To put the boys to bed, turn to *A Bedtime Story* on page 42.

To heat water, turn to *The Manger* on page 44.

A Bedtime Story

Tabitha offers to heat the water. You take Samuel and Jacob into the house. Jacob begins to cry. "Mama?"

You bend down and hug him. "She's helping Mary." The boys spread their sleeping mats on the floor.

"Shall I tell you a story?" you ask.

The boys nod.

"Many years ago a shepherd boy named David lived here in Bethlehem. His three older brothers were away at war. David's father, Jesse, told him to take food to his brothers. So David went to the battlefield. While he was there, he met a giant."

Samuel's eyes grow wide. "A giant?"

"Yes. A giant named Goliath. The giant had shiny armor and a huge iron sword. Everyone was afraid. David was just a simple shepherd boy. He was afraid too. But he said, 'The Lord will deliver me.' So David put his trust in God and fought the giant. And he won."

"I trust God too," Samuel says.

"Me, too," Jacob adds. The boys roll over and go to sleep.

Soon after, a shout rises from Tabitha's house. You hear singing. The women are welcoming the new baby.

Tabitha rushes in with the news. "It's a boy! A firstborn son! Mary wrapped him in cloths and laid him in a manger. I'm the one who put clean straw in the manger," Tabitha says proudly.

Oh, how you wish you could have been there! You rub Jacob's back. *I suppose I helped in a different way*, you tell yourself. "Did you see the baby?" you ask Tabitha.

"Oh, yes. He's tiny."

"I wish I could see him."

Mama walks in. "It's late. Mary is tired. Of course, I suppose if you are very quiet . . ."

"I'll be quiet."

Mama smiles gently. "I know you will. But it might be better to wait until morning. Would you girls like to climb to the roof and visit for a while?"

To see the baby now, turn to *Unexpected Visitors* on page 49.

To go to the roof, turn to *The Roof* on page 54.

The Manger

You begin heating water. Mama interrupts. "I'll do that," she says. "And I'll put the boys to bed. I want you and Tabitha to go to Tabitha's house and clean one of the mangers the animals use. Fill it with fresh hay. It will make a fine bed for Mary's baby."

Tabitha's house is crowded. You slip inside. Two stone mangers are set into the floor at the far end of the family room near the animals' pen. At night, the oxen can reach into the mangers and nibble on hay.

You clean the manger quickly. You fill it with fresh hay. Mary and Joseph sleep here, close to the mangers. "Mary told me that she likes hearing the oxen lowing in the night," Tabitha says.

You smile. "I like that too."

Mary gasps, and the baby cries for the very first time.

"It's a boy," the midwife says. "A firstborn son."

You're eager to see the baby. Someone must tell Joseph the news. Men are not allowed to be present at a birth. They are waiting at the home of Thaddeus, who works with Uncle Caleb.

To see the baby, turn to *A New Baby* on page 46.

To tell Joseph, turn to *A Message for Joseph* on page 48.

A New Baby

"I'll tell Joseph," Thaddeus's wife says. That means you can stay and see the baby.

You inch closer to the manger. He is tiny. Were you ever that small? Was Papa?

Susanna washes the baby with warm water. She rubs his tiny body with salt and olive oil. It will help him grow strong and healthy. Mary wraps him in clean cloths and lays him in the manger. She tucks a blanket around him.

"The manger makes a fine bed," Mary says.

Your heart swells with pride.

It's been an exciting night. You and Tabitha stumble across the courtyard and go to bed. You don't hear a thing.

In the morning Mama says, "We had visitors last night. You were sleeping. Shepherds came from the hills to see the baby. They said angels sent them."

"Angels?"

Mama nods. "Everyone is talking about it. But we must get back to work. It is past time to go to the well. And your father left his cloak behind. It is getting cold."

To go to the well, turn to *At the Well* on page 58.

To take Papa his cloak, turn to *At Papa's Shop* on page 59.

A Message for Joseph

Thaddeus lives nearby. It only takes a minute to reach his home. You ask for Papa and tell him the news. "I'll tell Joseph," he says. "Now run along home."

It is late. When you reach home, Aunt Martha asks you and Tabitha to walk Susanna home.

The streets are dark. Susanna is happy to have company.

It doesn't take long to reach Susanna's house. She lights a lamp and offers you honey cake. Will Mama be worried?

To return home, turn to *Hurry Home* on page 51.

To stay for cake, turn to *Cake* on page 56.

Unexpected Visitors

"Let's go see the baby," you say.

Tabitha leads the way. You slip inside and tiptoe to the manger. The baby is sleeping. "He's sweet," you say.

"He's a gift from God," Mary says. She smiles at you. Joseph stands nearby.

Suddenly there's a knock at the door. Uncle Caleb answers. He steps outside. A minute later he comes back and speaks to Joseph.

Joseph nods. "Let them in."

Rough-looking men enter. You know them. They are shepherds. They gather around the manger and bow their heads. Some kneel.

An older shepherd says, "We were watching our flocks in the hills. Suddenly a bright light appeared and an angel spoke. We were afraid. But the angel said: 'Fear not: for, behold, I bring you good tidings of great joy, which shall be to all people. For unto you is born this day in the city of David a Savior, which is Christ the Lord.

And this shall be a sign unto you; Ye shall find the babe wrapped in swaddling clothes, lying in a manger.'

"So we came here. We came to find the baby, the Savior."

Can it be true? Did angels announce this baby's birth?

The shepherd says more. "We are simple shepherds. But the angels came to us. They said that God sent Christ the Lord for all people."

You hold Tabitha's hand. You are both quiet, thinking about what you have heard. You slip home to bed. But it is hard to sleep. You are too excited.

"I believe them," Tabitha whispers. "Do you?"

To say you believe, turn to *"I Believe"* on page 71.

To doubt their story, turn to *"It's Hard to Believe"* on page 72.

Hurry Home

"Mama will be worried. We must get home."

Mama hugs you when you return. "You did well tonight," she says. You beam brighter than the oil lamp that lights the room. The boys are sleeping. You are too excited to go to bed.

"Can we go see the baby?"

"Not tonight," Mama says. "Mary is tired. She needs to rest."

"Tomorrow?"

Mama nods.

During the next few weeks, you often see Mary and the baby. He is growing quickly. When he is forty days old, it is time to go to the temple. Mary and Joseph will offer a sacrifice in honor of the baby. Tabitha's family is going. So is yours.

It is safest to travel in a group. The roads are dangerous. Robbers swoop down from the hills and attack travelers. Roman soldiers patrol the roads. Their shiny helmets and sharp swords scare you.

You leave at first light. It takes two hours to reach the Jerusalem city gate. Tall walls surround the city. They have stood for hundreds of years. They protect Jerusalem. Roman soldiers stand guard too.

You enter through a big wooden gate. There is so much to see. Farmers carry vegetables and fruits. Children chase one another. Several old men toss dice in games of chance. You stop at a stall selling perfumes. They smell lovely. You linger by a display of silk shawls. How beautiful!

Suddenly you look up. Where is Tabitha? Where is Mama? You have fallen behind.

A small child darts in front of you. She trips and tumbles. She is just a baby. You want to stop to help her, but Mama is nearly out of sight. If you don't hurry, you'll lose her. It is dangerous to get lost in such a big city.

To help the girl, turn to *A Helping Hand* on page 61.

To follow Mama, turn to *The Lost Sheep* on page 63.

The Roof

The roof? What a good idea. You climb the stairs to the flat roof. On hot summer nights, you sleep here. It is cool tonight. You draw your cloak around you. "Look at the stars," you say. "They're beautiful!"

Tabitha settles down beside you. "Count them," she says. You begin counting, but Tabitha interrupts. "Shh! Do you hear something?"

You listen. It is the *slap-slap* of sandals on the street. "Someone is coming. Who could be out so late? Soldiers? Tax collectors? Troublemakers?"

There's no shortage of trouble these days. Roman soldiers and tax collectors prowl the streets.

Tabitha peers into the night. "They look like shepherds. And they're stopping at my house. Let's go see what they want."

Tabitha starts down the stairs.

"Wait!" you call. "Maybe they are really soldiers dressed like shepherds?"

Tabitha laughs. "That's silly."

To go with Tabitha, turn to *Spying* on page 64.

To hold Tabitha back, turn to *A Big Thud* on page 66.

Cake

"I love cake!" The sweet cake melts in your mouth.

"I baked it for my nephew." Susanna's nephew is a shepherd, like her husband. They watch over the flocks in the hills above Bethlehem. Just as you take the last bite of your cake, the door swings open.

"Eli!" Susanna cries. "What a surprise!"

It's Susanna's husband. He is not alone. Many shepherds are with him. "We've come to see if a baby has been born in Bethlehem tonight."

Susanna steps outside to speak with Eli. A few minutes later, she summons you and Tabitha.

"These men want to speak with your father, Tabitha. Go with them."

What could shepherds want with Uncle Caleb? You do as Susanna asks and go with them. You step aside as Eli knocks on Uncle Caleb's door.

Uncle Caleb comes outside.

"Come," Tabitha whispers.

"No. Let's wait and see what they want," you say.

Turn to *Spying* on page 64.

At the Well

You carry the water jug to the well. Everyone is talking about the angels' visit.

"Did you see the baby?" someone asks.

"Oh, yes. He's a fine boy."

"But he's just a boy," an old woman says. "Every mother thinks her child is special. But this one is no more special than the next. God's son would not be born to the wife of a poor carpenter. He would not be born in Bethlehem. No. He would be born in a palace to a queen."

You nod. She's probably right. "But wouldn't it be wonderful if Mary's baby is Christ the Lord?"

"Yes. It would," the old woman admits. "It would be a miracle."

THE END

At Papa's Shop

Papa's shop is not far. You are nearly there when you hear someone shout. "Move aside!"

Someone else speaks, but you cannot hear his words.

"He said move," another voice shouts.

You round the corner. Two boys jump another boy. They pound him with their fists.

You run toward the shop. "Papa! Come quickly!"

"What's wrong?"

"A fight!" you say.

Papa pulls the boys apart. You recognize the twins. Their father owns the vineyard. They are troublemakers.

"Go home," Papa tells the twins. They slink away. They spit on the shepherd boy as they leave. You know him. He's Susanna's nephew.

Blood runs down the boy's cheek. He wipes it away.

"It could have been worse," Papa says, helping the boy up. A broken jug lies nearby.

Papa gives him a new one. "Everyone has heard of the angels' visit," Papa says. "Some people feel jealous. 'Why shepherds?' they ask. 'Why not us?' But no one can understand the mind of God. Go in peace. God be with you."

"And with you," the boy says.

Papa takes the cloak from you. "Something wonderful happened last night," he says. "That boy saw angels. His faith is strong. We must accept the ways of the Lord. 'For my thoughts are not your thoughts, neither are your ways my ways, saith the Lord.'"

Papa's words make you smile. You hurry home to finish the day's work.

THE END

A Helping Hand

Helping is the right thing to do. You bend down and lift the little girl up. You wipe away her tears and brush the dust off her gown. It is made of the finest silk. Someone has embroidered flowers around the edges.

A Roman soldier marches towards you. He wears a red cloak and black bands around his wrists. He is a centurion, an officer in the Roman army. You shiver. Roman soldiers are dangerous. Their leaders are the most dangerous of all.

To run away, turn to *Finding Mama* on page 69.

To face the centurion, turn to *Nothing to Fear* on page 77.

The Lost Sheep

A woman rushes over to help the little girl. You dash off. A minute later you catch up with Mama.

"Here's my little lost sheep," Mama says. "God kept you safe."

You enter the massive temple gate. The walls gleam with gold. The temple is the most beautiful building in the world.

The temple is crowded. People mill about. Some pray. Others bring sacrifices. Everyone wants God's blessing. Mary and Joseph buy two doves for a sacrifice to the Lord. Today the baby will be presented to God. A priest offers blessings.

Soon it is time to leave. You reach home before darkness falls. Jerusalem is an exciting city. Bethlehem is a quiet little village. But you love it. God must love it too. After all, he chose Bethlehem as the birthplace of the Savior.

THE END

Spying

Tabitha will not wait. So you follow her. You slip into her house through the small gate used to bring the animals in and out. The animals are wakeful. The animal pen makes a perfect place to spy. You can see everything, but no one can see you.

A single lamp lights the family room. Mary and Joseph have their backs to you. The baby is lying in the manger. Is he sleeping?

Tabitha puts a finger to her lips. She points to the shepherds. They are standing beside the manger. Some kneel. They wear heavy wool cloaks. Some carry staffs. Others have rods tied to their sashes. You look at their rough faces. They are smiling. Their eyes shine with great joy.

They bow to Mary and Joseph. And then they leave.

You and Tabitha slip outside.

"Why did they come?" you ask. But Tabitha has no answers.

The next day you learn something amazing. Angels visited the shepherds in the fields and told them to come. The angels said that the baby was a gift from God. They called him a Savior, Christ the Lord.

Everyone is talking about it. Some believe the shepherds. Many do not.

To believe the shepherds, turn to *"I Believe"* on page 71.

To doubt their story, turn to *"It's Hard to Believe"* on page 72.

A Big Thud

Tabitha agrees to wait. But not for long. When she starts down the stairs, you reach out to grab her cloak. She slips from your grasp. You reach out again. But this time, you stumble and lose your footing. You tumble down the stairs.

"Aaah!" You land with a thud in the courtyard. "My ankle! My ankle!"

Papa rushes out. He carries you inside. The ankle is badly twisted. Mama wraps cloths around it. "It will heal," she says. She gives you some herbs for the pain.

By morning it is badly swollen. You cannot walk. Mama helps you to the courtyard. You grind grain for bread. You weave cloth. It is a long, boring day.

Tabitha stops by after supper. She tells you about the shepherds. "They came to see the baby. An angel told them that they would find a baby wrapped in cloths and lying in a manger. The angel called him Lord."

"Mary's baby?"

Tabitha nods.

"Is it possible?"

Your ankle heals quickly. You visit Mary and her baby. Mary and Joseph will name him Yeshua. In Greek, he will be called Jesus. You hold the baby. He looks up at you. You rock him and sing to him. He falls asleep in your arms. You love Mary's baby.

When Jesus is forty days old, Mary and Joseph take baby Jesus to the temple in Jerusalem. They will offer a sacrifice to the Lord. It is the custom when a child is born.

Tabitha's family is going to the temple with them. You go too.

Going to Jerusalem is exciting. You enter through a large wooden gate. The streets are crowded. Uncle Caleb says that 60,000 people live in Jerusalem! It looks like most of them are at the temple. The temple courtyard is so crowded.

A man named Simeon walks up to Mary and Joseph.

"May I hold the baby?"

He takes the child in his arms. He praises God. He blesses Joseph, Mary, and the baby. And then he tells Mary, "This child is set for the fall and rising again of many in Israel."

His words confuse and frighten you. You wish Mama were here to explain. Tabitha clings to Aunt Martha. You move as close as you can.

"Don't be afraid," Aunt Martha says. "Simeon is a prophet. His message is from God. Look at Mary."

Mary is smiling. Joy lights her face.

An old woman steps forward. She says that Jesus is the promised Savior.

"Who is she?" you ask.

"Anna," Aunt Martha says. "She never leaves the temple. She worships night and day."

After the priest blesses the baby, you begin the journey home. You have much to think about. Will you tell Mama what Simeon and Anna said?

To tell Mama, turn to *Telling Mama* on page 73.

To remain silent, turn to *Remembering* on page 75.

Finding Mama

You set the child down and run. You stop beside a market stall to catch your breath. You risk a look back. The centurion is holding the child. He is smiling. Is he her father?

You have to find Mama and the others. The golden roofs of the temple rise above Jerusalem. You go directly there. Everyone is waiting at the temple gate.

"What happened?" Tabitha asks. "We thought we had lost you."

You enter the court of the women. This is where the baby Jesus will be presented to God. The ceremony is brief. The priest gives thanks for the child's birth. Mary and Joseph give two doves as an offering.

As you are leaving, an old man approaches Mary and Joseph. He takes the baby in his arms and blesses him.

You and Tabitha slip outside. "Who was that?"

"Papa called him Simeon," Tabitha says. "He is a prophet."

It's a quiet walk home. Everyone seems lost in thought.

Soon life returns to normal. The people who came for the census return home. You return to daily tasks. So does everyone else.

Over time you forget about the baby, the angels, and the shepherds. Maybe someday you'll remember. Maybe someday you'll understand that you were part of a miracle—the birth of Christ the Lord.

THE END

"I Believe"

"I believe too," you say.

Tabitha smiles. "Mary and Joseph will name the baby Jesus. It means *one who saves*. He is just a tiny baby, but someday he will save us all."

Over the years, you often think about the baby Jesus. Mary, Joseph, and their child left Bethlehem many years ago. But you hear rumors about a rabbi named Jesus. He makes people who are blind see. He makes people who are deaf hear. Is he the child of Mary and Joseph? Is he the savior that the angels promised?

THE END

"It's Hard to Believe"

"It's hard to believe," you tell Tabitha.

At first you are excited by the shepherds' story. Everyone is talking about it. But Bethlehem is a busy town. People have work to do. Soon the shepherds' story is old news. How could a tiny baby save God's people?

Over time you forget about the shepherds and the angels. But you never forget the baby. You remember his gentle mother. You try to be as loving and kind to others as Mary was to you.

THE END

Telling Mama

You don't say anything right away. You need time to think.

The next evening Mama is alone in the courtyard. You tell her what Simeon and Anna said.

"Do you believe that the baby is special?" you ask. "Could he be the Savior?"

"All children are special." Mama smiles gently. "Especially a firstborn son. But do you really believe that God would send His Savior to this poor village?"

You smile. It seems like a silly idea.

"Of course not," Mama says. "Do not trouble yourself. Leave such concerns to the high priests. They will know the promised Savior when they see him."

Mama is always right. Even so, you often remember those days. You saw shepherds worship a baby in a manger. You heard prophets call him *Savior*. You'll always believe that God did something special that night. Perhaps someday you'll learn the truth.

THE END

Remembering

You say nothing to Mama. But you think about it often. The baby looked like other babies. He cried. He ate. He needed to be washed. But angels don't announce every birth. Shepherds don't visit every baby. Prophets don't declare all children *Saviors*.

Mama says that God is all-powerful. Is God powerful enough to use a baby to save the world?

Samuel and Jacob run into the yard. They are growing quickly. Baby Jesus will grow too.

Soon Bethlehem returns to normal. The shepherds return to the hills. Visitors go home. People stop talking about Mary, Joseph, and their baby Jesus.

But you remember. Many years later when your first son is born, you think of Mary and her firstborn son. Where are they now?

By the time your first grandchild is born, you hear rumors of a new teacher named Jesus. Jesus? He heals the sick. Some say he brings the dead back to life. Could this be the child born on that long-ago night?

You smile. God is good!

THE END

Nothing to Fear

You have not done anything wrong. You stand firm holding the child in your arms. Slowly you raise your eyes and look at the centurion.

He is smiling. He reaches out for the little girl. "My daughter," he says in your language, Aramaic. He speaks with a Roman accent, but you understand him. "You were kind to help. Thank you."

What a relief! He wasn't angry. He was worried.

You look for your family. They are nowhere in sight.

"Is something wrong?" the centurion asks.

"My family," you say. "I'm afraid that I lost them."

"Where are you going?" he asks.

"To the temple."

"Do not worry. We will take you there." He sets his daughter down and takes her hand in his own. "It is not far," the centurion says. He guides you along the dusty streets to the temple.

Mama is waiting by the temple gate. You rush toward her and then stop to thank the Roman.

"It is I who must thank you," he says. "Be well."

It has been a time of miracles: the baby, the shepherds, the angels, and, most surprising of all, a kind centurion. You say a prayer of thanks: "For the Lord is good; his mercy is everlasting; and his truth endureth to all generations."

THE END

The Boy from Parthia

Father knows everything there is to know about camels. He owns hundreds of them. Father's camels are fast. They are strong. They carry heavy loads across rough country. Today a group of Magi, or wise men, hired Father to take them on a long journey.

"We will be gone for many months—perhaps a year," Father says. "We will follow a star to the West."

"A star?" Mother asks.

"Yes. The Magi are watching a new star. It rises in the east as the sun sets in the west. They believe it tells of the birth of a new king, a king of the Jews. If so, it may mean the end of Roman rule."

"That is good news," Mother says. The Romans are a threat. Their armies have invaded Palestine, Arabia, Parthia, and beyond. They want to control the entire world.

Father turns to you. "I thought you would help me with the camels. But perhaps not. Pakur, one of the youngest Magi, is seeking a clerk. He

wants someone who can read Aramaic. I told him that you could do it."

Aramaic is the common language of the whole region.

"So he has offered you the job. If you take it, I will hire someone else to tend the camels."

This is the first time Father has given you a choice. It's a sign of his trust.

To become a clerk, turn to *The Clerk* on page 82.

To tend the camels, turn to *Preparing for the Journey* on page 88.

The Clerk

Father is proud that you are good at reading and arithmetic. He will be pleased if you take the job. You agree to become Pakur's clerk.

Working for one of the wise men of Parthia sounds exciting. You've never met a Magus before, but you've certainly heard stories about them. The Magi interpret dreams. They predict the future. Many years ago, they were kings in northwest Persia. Now Persia is part of the huge Parthian Empire. The Magi advise the king. Some are priests. Others are noblemen. Even the Jews in faraway Palestine respect the Magi.

You wonder what he will expect of you? Will you stay with Father or with Pakur? Father calms your fears. "Do not worry. Pakur is a good man. You will stay in his tent. We will camp at khans whenever possible."

Khans are inns for caravans. They have high walls and strong doors to keep robbers outside. Travelers pitch tents inside the walls. The camels and other animals stay inside the walls too.

Pakur greets you warmly. "Can you run fast and read well?" he asks.

"Oh, yes. I win races. I like to read."

"Then you will be a fine clerk. You will do errands too."

Pakur puts you to work packing for the journey. You place several reed pens and ink in a special wooden box. There are scrolls in the box too. Another box holds maps. Another has charts of the sky.

Pakur buys gold. Caravans from South Arabia bring frankincense and myrrh. Pakur explains how the farmers harvest frankincense. "They slash the thin bark of the Boswellia tree. They say that the tree cries. The tears harden into yellow beads. When the beads are warmed, they give off a sweet smell."

"Father says that frankincense carries prayers to heaven," you say.

Pakur smiles. "It may be so. Myrrh also comes from trees. Myrrh trees produce a yellow gum that is used as oil and or perfume. It helps with pain too. These three—frankincense, myrrh, and gold—are the most precious gifts in the entire world."

The caravan is nearly ready to leave.

"There is one more errand," Pakur says. "The tailor has finished my new silk robe." He tells you the tailor's name. "Do you know how to get to his shop?"

You don't know where it is. But you fear that if you tell the truth, Pakur will send you home.

To admit you don't know, turn to *Telling the Truth* on page 85.

To say that you do know, turn to *A Costly Lie* on page 87.

Telling the Truth

You tell the truth. "I do not know where it is."

Pakur gives you directions. "It is not far," he says.

You find the shop and pick up the silk robe within an hour.

It's time to begin the journey. It takes more than one hundred camels to carry everything. There are chests filled with gold, frankincense, and myrrh. There are Magi, clerks, cooks, and camel tenders. Many will ride on the camels. Armed soldiers on horseback guard the caravan from robbers.

Travel by camel is slow. You cross the Syrian Desert. At Palmyra, you camp near an oasis. Other caravans camp there too. Some carry silk from China or cotton from India. Others haul spices. Ships will take the spices to Rome.

At night, the Magi watch the skies. "The star is leading us to Jerusalem."

You cross the Jordan River and stop in Jericho.

"We must consult Herod the Great," the Magi say. The Romans have put Herod in charge of Judea.

"He's a tyrant," one Magus says. "He killed his first wife and two of his sons. The Roman emperor said he would rather be a pig than Herod's son."

Everyone laughs.

At dusk two days later the caravan reaches Jerusalem and stops at a khan.

"Where is the star?" someone asks. It is no longer visible in the night sky.

"Tomorrow we will visit Herod's palace," Pakur tells you. "You may come along. Or perhaps you'd rather use the time to visit your father."

To go to Herod's palace, turn to *Herod's Palace* on page 91.

To stay at the khan, turn to *Visit with Father* on page 93.

A Costly Lie

"I know that place," you say. But it's a lie. You hope you can find the shop. You ask people in the streets. No one can help. At last a kind old man points it out. By the time you reach the tailor's shop, it is closed. You return without the robe.

"You should have told the truth. I could have given you directions," Pakur said. "Now I fear I cannot trust you. If I cannot trust you, you are of no use to me."

You have no choice but to return home and beg Father's forgiveness.

"It was not meant to be," Father says. "You will help me tend the camels. The work is hard. I trust you will not ever lie to me."

"No, Father. I know better. You can trust me."

Turn to *Preparing for the Journey* on page 88.

Preparing for the Journey

You enjoy working with the camels. Someday you will lead caravans. Someday you will own one hundred camels of your own. Maybe more.

Mother bakes a special kind of dry bread for the journey. It will keep for weeks. She packs beans, pine nuts, and spices. They will make a tasty stew. "Buy vegetables and fruit along the way," she says.

You help father oil the saddles. Each camel will carry a rider or supplies. They'll carry food, tents, and the Magi's treasures—gold, frankincense, and myrrh.

"Gold is heavy. Will it be too heavy?" you ask.

"No," Father says. "Do not worry. Each camel can carry up to six hundred pounds."

When everything is ready, Father prods the camels into line behind his donkey. Camels are good followers. Wherever the donkey goes, they will follow.

The Magi, their servants, the cooks, and the camel tenders are assigned camels of their own. Some ride donkeys. The Parthian cavalry ride the finest horses. Several merchants join the caravan. "There is safety in numbers," one says.

Ibil, the camel you ride, has a lumpy back. He spits. He is a noisy fellow too. All camels are. They moan, groan, bellow, and roar. Sometimes

they make high bleating sounds. They can even growl like giant cats.

You cross the sandy desert. Soon you enter scrubland. Father calls it the badlands. Few plants grow here. The caravan makes music. Men shout to one another. Jars and jugs bang against each other. Winds whistle through desert canyons, and vultures screech overhead.

At night you stop at khans. They are protected courtyards where you can pitch a tent. Some nights there are no khans. Then you camp in the open. Guards protect the caravan from robbers.

You rise early and travel until sunset. It is dark by the time you unload the camels. You set up tents and build campfires. The Magi have their own fires nearby. You join the camel tenders around Father's campfire. Guards circle the camp.

One night a shout wakes you. You jump up. "Stay here!" Father yells as he ducks out of the tent.

To rush after him, turn to *Trying to Help* on page 94.

To obey father, turn to *Obeying Father* on page 97.

Herod's Palace

You go with the Magi to see Herod's palace. Jerusalem is a big city. It's home to about 60,000 people. The streets are crowded. The Magi look like kings in their brightly colored robes. People stare and move aside.

Herod's palace is built of yellow bricks. They shimmer like gold.

A guard meets you at the gate. "Wait here," he says. "I'll call a priest."

The priest arrives. "Welcome. How can I help you?"

The Chief Magus steps forward. "We have come to worship the new king of the Jews. Where is he? We have followed his star."

"Herod is the king of the Jews," the priest says.

"We believe there is another, a child," the Chief Magus says.

"I will speak with Herod," the priest says. "Come back later."

The Magi leave.

Pakur gives you two silver coins. "I'm going to the temple. I have heard that it is very beautiful. You can come too. Or you can visit the marketplace. Merchants sell many fine items there."

To go to the temple, turn to *The Jerusalem Temple* on page 105.

To go to the market, turn to *The Market* on page 107.

Visit with Father

"I will visit Father."

You have not seen much of him during the trip. He is with the camels. It is good to spend time together. One of the biggest camels nuzzles your hair while you talk.

Pakur returns with news. "We could not see Herod, so we left a message. We must wait for an answer. This is a good time for you to tour the city. Go to the market or go explore the whole city."

To see other sites, turn to *Exploring the City* on page 101.

To go to the market, turn to *The Market* on page 107.

Trying to Help

You want to help. You grab your bow and a good supply of arrows and rush into the night. A guard gallops by. "We're under attack!" he shouts. "Protect yourself!"

Men run wildly through the camp. They shout and scream at one another. It is hard to tell who is friend and who is not. Where is Father?

You run toward the tents of the Magi. Someone rushes toward you. He's about your size. Can you tackle him? Can you knock him to the ground? Or should you shoot him with your bow and arrow?

To shoot him, turn to *Ready to Shoot* on page 95.

To tackle him, turn to *Attack* on page 98.

Ready to Shoot

You lift your bow and arrow to shoot when a Magus runs out of the tent. "Don't shoot! That's my clerk."

You lower the bow.

The clerk points to your right. "There!"

As you turn a man hurls a rock at the Magus. You nock the arrow, aim, and shoot. The arrow pierces the robber's arm. He staggers away.

The thieves run off.

"They won't be back," a guard says.

The Magus thanks you for your help. "You saved my life!"

The journey continues. You cross rough desert lands. The camel tenders tell stories, sing, and joke with one another around the campfire. Guards keep troublemakers away. In the mornings, you load packs on the camels. The work makes you thirsty. You go to the well for a drink.

One morning, as you scoop water into your hands and drink it, you hear a strange huffing and puffing sound.

You stop and listen. The desert is a dangerous place. Has a child fallen into the well? Is a sick camel struggling to breathe?

To check it out, turn to *Checking for Danger* on page 100.

To ignore the sound, turn to *Staying Safe* on page 103.

Obeying Father

You do as Father says. He will never trust you if you disobey. A mounted guard gallops by. "We're under attack!" he shouts.

You'll do your part, even if you can't leave the tent. You stand in the tent door with your bow and arrow. You can shoot if danger comes near.

A man stumbles toward you.

"Don't shoot!" he yells.

"Father!" You toss down the bow and run toward him.

"The guards chased the bandits away. All is well."

The journey continues. One night you hear two camel handlers shouting.

"It's a fight," someone shouts. The men face each other. These are rough men. Fights are common.

"Help me stop this before someone gets hurt," a guard yells.

To keep a safe distance, turn to *Staying Safe* on page 103.

To help break up the fight, turn to *A Cruel Cut* on page 114.

Attack

You toss your bow to the ground and race toward the boy. You crash into him. He lands on his back. You sit on him and hold his arms down. "I've caught you now, thief!"

A young Magus rushes over. "He's no thief! He's my clerk. Let him up!"

A clerk? You help him up and brush the dust from his robe.

"I'm sorry."

"Hurry! Inside." The Magus pulls you both into his tent. A large man lies near several chests.

"This is the thief. He tried to steal our treasures. My clerk knocked him out. Find a guard," the Magus says.

It only takes a minute to find a guard. He hauls the thief away.

The Magus thanks you. His clerk scowls and rubs his head.

The rest of the journey is calm. You cross the Jordan River at Jericho. From there you go south toward Jerusalem. You stop at a large khan just outside the city gates.

You want to explore the great city, but Father shakes his head.

Turn to *City Dangers* on page 117.

Checking for Danger

It will only take a minute to see what is making the noise. The sound grows louder. It is coming from some rocks near an acacia tree. It's not a child. It's not a camel. But you are curious. What is it?

You pick up a stick and poke it at the rocks. You never see the snake until it strikes. It waits, huffing and puffing, until you get close. Then it lifts its head and strikes. It sinks its fangs into your hand.

You cry out in surprise. Your hand is already swelling.

People come running.

"An adder!" someone yells. The snake slithers away.

Someone runs to find Father.

You fall to the ground, too dizzy to stand. Your lips and tongue swell. You cannot breathe. "Father," you wheeze. "Father."

It is your last word. Your journey ends in the desert halfway to Jerusalem.

THE END

Exploring the City

It will be fun to explore the city on your own. You walk quickly through the Tower Gate and past the Antonia Fortress. Its high towers overlook the countryside.

The streets are crowded. People are going to work, to market, or to the temple. Soldiers push their way through the crowds.

The marble walls of the temple rise to a great height. You rush past. After all, you are a Gentile, and this is the worship place of the Jews. You walk along straight, narrow streets lined with large houses. Beautiful gardens surround them. You walk on twisting, narrow streets. Poor people live here. Their houses are smaller.

Craftsmen work in open-air shops. They make pottery, jewelry, clothing, and furniture. You join some boys in a game of marbles.

When the sun begins to set, you return to the khan. "We're going to Bethlehem," Pakur says. "It's a small village south of here."

For the next several hours, you saddle camels and load supplies onto their backs.

Turn to *The Star Returns* on page 112.

Staying Safe

Father has taught you that it's wise to be careful. "Stay away from trouble," he says. "Let others break up fights. And in the desert, watch out for deadly creatures. You never know what dangers lurk beneath rocks."

So you decide to return to work. There's plenty to do.

The caravan continues its journey across the desert. You cross the Jordan River. "We are now in Judea," Father says. "In another day or two we will see Jerusalem."

The next day, you gaze into the distance. There! The gleaming walls of Jerusalem rise toward the sky. Father stops at a khan near the city gate. The camels munch thorny bushes.

The next morning the Magi go into the city. "I'd like to see the city too," you say.

Father is worried. "It's a dangerous place. I suppose you could go to the market for an hour."

You have some coins in your purse. It might be fun to see the market. Why is Father worried?

To go to the market, turn to *The Market* on page 107.

To ask Father to explain, turn to *City Dangers* on page 117.

The Jerusalem Temple

A Roman soldier watches as you pass by. "The soldiers are worried," Pakur says. "King Herod and the Romans fear a Jewish rebellion. They think we have come to encourage it."

You laugh. The Magi have no such plans.

"Look. There's the temple."

Herod's temple is famous throughout the world. It is the most beautiful building you have ever seen. Its marble walls shimmer. Lines of blue, green, and red run through the marble.

"Are we allowed to enter?" you ask.

"Yes," Pakur says. "Even though we are not Jews, we can enter the temple courtyard."

A golden gate leads to the courtyard. It is a busy place. Some people are praying. Others are visiting together. After you look around, Pakur says it is time to leave. "We must see if Herod has sent an answer."

The other Magi are waiting at the khan for Pakur. "Herod wants to see us in secret. We will leave Jerusalem after the meeting."

To see Herod, turn to *Seeing Herod* on page 109.

To prepare for the journey, turn to *Packing for the Trip* on page 110.

The Market

You set off for the market. You enter the city through the Essene Gate. Roman soldiers armed with swords march through the streets. About 60,000 people live in Jerusalem. Even more people visit on market day.

Merchants sell fabrics, perfumes, and jewelry under colorful tents. Weavers, carpenters, and jewelers work in open-air shops. So do potters and bakers. Newly picked grapes and olives, fresh cheeses, salted fish, fried locusts, and pastries tempt you. What treats! The sweet smell of fresh bread makes you hungry. Your stomach rumbles.

You buy three pomegranates, a cluster of grapes, and some cheese. A woman offers some food that is new to you. "What is it?" you ask, but you do not understand her answer.

She pushes it toward you. "Try," she says. You take a bite. It's delicious. You pay her. Then you sit on a low wall eating.

Suddenly you feel unwell. "My stomach," you groan. You double over. Standing up is impossible. You grasp your stomach and collapse onto the street.

Someone carries you inside. You wake in a stranger's bed. A woman offers you water. You take a sip before falling back to sleep. What is wrong? Could it be something you ate? For several days, you linger between sleeping and waking. Your fever rises and falls.

Finally you feel better. A kind Jewish woman took you in. She cared for you. You give her your remaining coins. It is not much—about what a vineyard worker earns for a day's work. "Thank you," she says. It does not begin to repay her kindness.

You return to the khan. Father's caravan is gone.

"They went to Bethlehem," the khan owner says. "They will be back."

To go to Bethlehem, turn to *On to Bethlehem* on page 111.

To wait in Jerusalem, turn to *Left Behind* on page 115.

Seeing Herod

"I will go with you." You're eager to see Herod's palace.

What a beautiful place it is! It is decorated in pure gold. The Magi bow before the king.

Herod remains seated. He looks ill. "When did this star first appear?" he asks.

The Magi answer.

Herod says that prophets have written about this child. "He will be born in Bethlehem. Go and make a careful search for the child. When you find him, report back to me. I want to worship him too."

"We shall leave this very night," the Chief Magus says.

Go to *The Star Returns* on page 112.

Packing for the Trip

"I'll pack for the trip," you say.

Pakur approves. "We are close now," he says. "Tell your father to get the camels ready to leave."

You help Father prepare to leave. You look up. The star that led you here no longer shines. What does that mean?

Pakur returns after dark. "Herod told us to go to Bethlehem. We are to find the child and report back to him. He wants to worship the child too."

What a surprise! Herod wants to worship the baby king.

Go to *The Star Returns* on page 112.

On to Bethlehem

You walk to Bethlehem alone. Olive trees and wheat fields surround the town. There's a potter's shop at the edge of the village. You stop and ask about the caravan.

The potter does not understand you.

"Magi?" you say.

He nods. "They were here. They left."

"Left?"

The potter shrugs. He doesn't know more.

You have no choice. You return to Jerusalem. The caravan may return there too.

Turn to *Left Behind* on page 115.

The Star Returns

Bethlehem is about two hours to the southwest. You haven't gone far when Pakur cries, "The star! It has returned!"

The star leads the way to a small village. People step outside and stare as the camels pass. A small girl waves. A little boy calls out.

The camels plod through the narrow streets. The star guides the Magi to a small house.

They knock on the door. "Come in," a young woman calls.

The Magi enter and drop to their knees before a small child and his mother.

This is the king? He looks like your baby brother.

Pakur calls for the gifts. It takes many servants to carry the chests of gold, frankincense, and myrrh into the house.

"For you," the Chief Magus says. And then the Magi leave.

The child's mother smiles. What will she do with these treasures?

Neighbors gather at the door. They want to see what is going on. If this village is like yours, they will gossip about this for years to come.

You camp outside the village.

During the night, Pakur wakes from a dream. "We must return by a different route," he says.

Other Magi had dreams too. "We must not go to Herod," they say.

And so you begin the trip home by another route. Every night, you look to the heavens. The star that led you to Bethlehem is gone. Who sent it? God? Why did the Magi visit this child?

The world is full of mysteries. Perhaps someday you will find the answers.

THE END

A Cruel Cut

Knife blades flash in the setting sun. You must protect Father's camels. You rush forward to help. One of the men raises his knife to stab the other. He stabs you instead.

You grab your chest. Blood stains your robe.

"What have I done? Forgive me!" the man cries.

Kind hands ease you to the ground. Faces swim above you. They look fuzzy. You look past the faces to the sky. A bright star hovers overhead. It's the star you've been following. Where will it take you? You reach for the star, close your eyes, and drift to sleep.

Father arrives. "Son!" he cries, and you open your eyes one last time.

"Father," you whisper. It is your last word. You die in the desert hundreds of miles from home.

THE END

Left Behind

You cannot find the caravan in Jerusalem. The owner of the khan says they never returned. "Perhaps they went home by a different route."

"Perhaps."

At first you are angry. Why did they leave me? Then you realize that Father trusts you. He knows you'll make your own way home. It doesn't take you long to find a caravan going east. You are welcome to go with them. The return trip takes many months.

When you reach home, Father greets you warmly. "The Magi decided to leave by a different route. I prayed that you would return home safely. My prayers have been answered."

"What happened in Bethlehem?" you ask.

"The Magi gave their gifts to a young boy. They believe he has been sent by God to save the world. The child's parents are simple people. How could such a child become king?" Father shakes his head and begins to laugh.

You laugh too. Later you wonder if the Magi might be right after all. As you learned on your journey, life is full of surprises.

THE END

City Dangers

"Why do you worry?" you ask.

"Herod's soldiers are eager to pick fights. They don't care who ends up in their jails. Look," he says, pointing into the distance.

A dozen or so tall crosses stand on a nearby hillside. Bodies hang from the crossbars. It is a terrible sight. "What have they done?"

"Some are thieves. Others speak out against Herod. It is a painful way to die."

You are a stranger here. It is safer to stay with Father.

As night falls, the Magi return with news. "We are going to Bethlehem. Prophets say it is the birthplace of the Savior."

The caravan is smaller now. Only the Magi, their servants, and the guards remain. Father leads the caravan along a well-worn road out of the city.

As you move out, the Magi shout. "The star! It has returned to guide our way!"

The star glows brighter and brighter. It leads to Bethlehem. The camels plod through the dusty streets. The star shines above a small house.

The Magi knock. The door opens. The Magi go inside.

One of them returns. "Bring the treasure," he says.

You carry a chest inside. You set it in front of a small boy and his parents. The Magi lie on the floor. They are praying. Is this child the king?

Soon the Magi leave. Their eyes shine in the starlight. A few cry tears of joy.

"Let us camp at the edge of the town to-night," the Chief Magus says.

In the morning, he tells Father to take a different route back to Parthia. "I was told to do so in a dream," he says.

You return to Parthia.

Years pass. You become a caravan leader just like Father. You take many journeys. Your travels take you to China. You visit India. You never know that the child you visited became a great teacher. You do not know that he died on a cross. Or that he rose from the dead to sit at the right hand of God, His father, in heaven. You never know, but others do.

THE END

Going Farther

REAL-LIFE DECISIONS

Every day you make real-life decisions. You choose your friends. You choose how to act. You choose what to do.

Your most important decision is this: Will you follow Jesus?

If you say yes, you can begin:
Reading the Bible
Praying daily
Serving others
Going to church
Sharing the good news of Jesus Christ

You can ask God for help by praying:

Dear God,

Thank you for sending Jesus to show me the way I should live. Help me to use my time wisely. Help me to serve the Lord with gladness. Help me to make good choices every day of my life.

In Christ's name I pray.

Amen.

GLOSSARY

census: a count of people and their property

centurion: an officer in the Roman army

kinsman: a relative or family member

Magi (plural) : wise men who advised the kings of the ancient Parthian Empire and used the stars to predict the future

Magus (singular): one wise man as defined above

manger: a feeding box for animals

Messiah: the Savior; the leader God promised

midwife: a woman who helps other women give birth

Parthia: a large empire in the ancient Near East that includes present-day Iran, Iraq, Armenia, parts of Turkey, and several other nations in the region

sacrifice: an animal, plant, or human life offered as a gift to God

Savior: the leader that God promised He would send to save His people

sheepfold: a nighttime pen for sheep

sling: a weapon that hurls stones and is made of leather with a pocket and two long strings

FIND IT IN YOUR BIBLE

The stories in this book are based on events recorded in the Bible. Read them for yourself.

Joseph and Mary go to Bethlehem for the census in Luke 2:1, 3–5.

The baby is born in Luke 2:6–7.

An angel appears to the shepherds in Luke 2:8–14.

The shepherds go to see the baby in Luke 2:15–20.

Mary and Joseph take the baby to the temple in Luke 2:22–24.

Simeon sees baby Jesus in Luke 2:25–35.

Anna sees baby Jesus in Luke 2: 36–38.

The Magi visit Herod in Matthew 2:1–8.

The Magi visit Bethlehem in Matthew 2:9–13.

WHAT BIBLE EXPERTS SAY . . .

ABOUT ROMAN RULE

About sixty years before Jesus was born, Roman leaders gained control of the land of Israel, which included Galilee, Samaria, and Judea. (You can find the places mentioned in this book in a Bible atlas or on the maps in the back of your Bible. To find them online, search Google: enter the name of a place and add the word "map." Then click on images. The search should bring up several maps of Bible places.)

By the time Jesus was born, one in every four people on earth lived under Roman rule.[1] It was Caesar Augustus, the Roman emperor, who ordered a census, or count, of all the people. Joseph went to Bethlehem, the home of his ancestors, for the census.

---

[1]"The Roman Empire," *The Roman Empire in the First Century*, http://www.pbs.org/empires/romans/empire/index.html.

ABOUT TRAVEL IN BIBLE TIMES

Wealthy people and Roman officials traveled in chariots or wagons.[2] Traders and merchants used camels to carry goods from place to place. They traveled in large groups called caravans. But most people walked. Sometimes women and small children rode donkeys during long journeys.[3] Family and friends traveled together when possible.

The trip could be dangerous. Merchants, soldiers, and Jews on their way to the temple or to visit relatives traveled along the highways.[4] So did thieves.

Travelers like Mary and Joseph probably stayed with family or friends along the way. Sometimes they camped near springs or wells. Large caravans often stayed at inns called khans or caravansaries.[5] They were not like today's motels. Most had a walled courtyard with

---

[2]Pat Alexander, *The Lion Encyclopedia of the Bible: Life and Times, Meaning and Message—A Comprehensive Guide* (Tring, England: Lion, 1986), 251.

[3]Arthur W. Klinck and Erich H. Kiehl, *Everyday Life in Bible Times* (St. Louis: Concordia Publishing House, 1995), 111–112.

[4]Reader's Digest. *Jesus and His Times* (Pleasantville, NY: Reader's Digest, 1987), 15.

[5]Ibid., 20.

a strong door to keep out robbers or trouble-makers.[6] People pitched their tents inside the walls and shared the courtyard space with the animals. Khans were often about a day's travel apart.[7] The Magi probably stayed at khans on their journey to Bethlehem.

ABOUT THE GUEST ROOM MENTIONED IN THE NATIVITY STORY

Were you surprised that Mary and Joseph did not stop at an inn in Bethlehem? Bethlehem was too small to have an inn. In that day, people knew their family histories.[8] Joseph knew that his family was related to King David. David began life in Bethlehem. He spent his boyhood as a shepherd in the nearby hills.[9] Joseph probably had family still living in Bethlehem. But even if they had moved away, Joseph would have been welcomed back to his hometown.[10] So would Mary.

---

[6]Klinck, 114.

[7]Ward, 193.

[8]Geldenhuys 100. Norval Geldenhuys, *Commentary on the Gospel of Luke: The English Text* (Grand Rapids: Eerdmans, 1971), 100.

[9]"King David," *Jewish Virtual Library*, http://www.jewishvirtual-library.org/jsource/biography/David.html.

[10]Kenneth E. Bailey, *Jesus Through Middle Eastern Eyes: Cultural Studies in the Gospels* (Downer's Grove: IVP Academic, 2008), 26.

After all, she was expecting a baby. People are always eager to help pregnant women. Mary had family nearby too. Her cousin Elizabeth lived in a village a short distance away.[11]

Some Bible experts believe that the words of Luke 2:6–7 do not refer to an inn that is full. They refer to a home where the guest room is already in use. They believe that early Bible translators used the word for guest room at an inn by mistake. The guest room was in someone's home. This story is based on the idea that the guest room was in use. That's why Mary and Joseph stayed with the family in their main room. Animals, who stayed inside at night, would have been nearby. When you read your Bible, you will not find the word stable. The Bible does mention a manger used to feed animals. Many homes had the mangers inside the house for the animals.

ABOUT THE SHEPHERDS

The shepherds in the hills above Bethlehem probably herded sheep that belonged to the priests in Jerusalem's temple. Only perfect

[11]Ibid., 26.

lambs could be sacrificed to God in the temple. The shepherds protected the temple sheep day and night.[12]

ABOUT THE WISE MEN

Far away, in lands to the East, Magi studied the stars. They knew about ancient writings. These writings promised that God would send a Savior to the Jewish people. For them this star signaled the Savior's birth.

Bible experts do not agree on who these Magi were. Some think that the wise men were Arabian astrologers. Astrologers were men who used the stars to predict the future.[13] Others think the magi came from the Parthian Empire. (The Parthian Empire stretched from what is now eastern Turkey into eastern Iran.) The Magi, or wise men, advised Parthian kings and performed important ceremonies.[14]

No one today knows the Magi's names or how many there were. Some stories imagine a

---

[12]James C. Martin and others, *A Visual Guide to Gospel Events: Fascinating Insights into Where They Happened and Why* (Grand Rapids: Baker Books, 2010), 24.

[13]Bailey, 52–53.

[14]Martin, 112–114.

small group traveling to Bethlehem; others believe that thousands formed the caravan that came from the East. We'll never know all the details. What we do know is that they came a great distance to honor a child. They believed that he would become King of the Jews.

BIBLIOGRAPHY

Alexander, Pat. *The Lion Encyclopedia of the Bible*. Tring, England: Lion, 1986.

Bailey, Kenneth E. *Jesus Through Middle Eastern Eyes: Cultural Studies in the Gospels*. Downer's Grove: IVP Academic, 2008.

Beers, V. Gilbert. *The Victor Journey Through the Bible*. Wheaton: Victor Books, 1996.

Daniel-Rops, Henri. *Daily Life in the Time of Jesus*. New York: Hawthorn, 1962.

Dowley, Tim. *The Kregel Pictorial Guide to the Bible*. Grand Rapids: Kregel Publications, 2000.

Gardner, Joseph L. *Atlas of the Bible: An Illustrated Guide to the Holy Land*. Pleasantville, NY: Reader's Digest Association, Inc., 1981.

King, Philip J., and Lawrence E. Stager. *Life in Biblical Israel*. Louisville: Westminster John Knox Press, 2001.

Klinck, Arthur W., and Erich H. Kiehl. *Everyday Life in Bible Times*. St. Louis: Concordia Publishing House, 1995.

Levine, Amy-Jill, and Marc Zvi Brettler, eds. *The Jewish Annotated New Testament: New Revised Standard Version Bible Translation*. New York: Oxford University Press, 2011.

Martin, James C., John A. Beck, and David G. Hansen. *A Visual Guide to Gospel Events: Fascinating Insights into Where They Happened and Why*. Grand Rapids: Baker Books, 2010.

Reader's Digest. *Illustrated Dictionary of Bible Life and Times*. Pleasantville, NY: Reader's Digest, 1997.

Reader's Digest. *Jesus and His Times*. Pleasantville, New York: Reader's Digest, 1987.

Teringo, J. Robert. *The Land and People Jesus Knew: A Visual Tour of First-Century Palestine*. Minneapolis: Bethany House, 1985.

Thompson, J. A. *Handbook of Life in Bible Times*. Downer's Grove: InterVarsity Press, 1986.

Vamosh, Miriam Feinberg. *Daily Life at the Time of Jesus*. Herzlia, Israel: Palphot, 2007.